USBORNE HOTSHOTS

TENNIS

USBORNE HOTSHOTS
TENNIS

Anita Ganeri

Edited by Lisa Miles
Designed by Nigel Reece

*Illustrated by Joe McEwan, Kuo Kang Chen
and Guy Smith*

Photographs by Bob Martin (Allsport UK)

Series editor: Judy Tatchell
Series designer: Ruth Russell

*Models: Hedley Grist and
Ana Alvarez*

CONTENTS

The court

Today, tennis is played on many different surfaces, but all courts are rectangular and identical in size. The court is divided in two by the net, with markings to show the boundaries for both singles and doubles matches.

Zones of the court

Each half of the court can be divided into three playing areas, known as the backcourt, the forecourt and the midcourt, or "no-man's land". Avoid standing in no-man's land to receive shots. Your opponent will find it easy to catch you out.

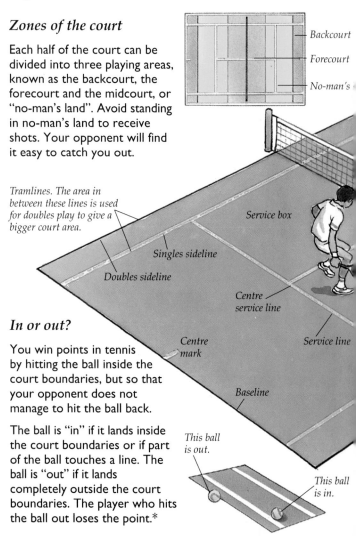

Backcourt

Forecourt

No-man's

Tramlines. The area in between these lines is used for doubles play to give a bigger court area.

Service box

Singles sideline

Doubles sideline

Centre service line

Service line

In or out?

You win points in tennis by hitting the ball inside the court boundaries, but so that your opponent does not manage to hit the ball back.

Centre mark

Baseline

The ball is "in" if it lands inside the court boundaries or if part of the ball touches a line. The ball is "out" if it lands completely outside the court boundaries. The player who hits the ball out loses the point.*

This ball is out.

This ball is in.

*See page 30 for how to score.

Crazy court

The hour-glass shaped court on the right was used for the 19th century game of "sticky". The net was stretched across the narrowest part of the court.

Right court

Left court

Net cord. If a service hits the net cord but lands in, a "let" is called. You can replay the service.

A service from the left-hand side of the court must land in the right-hand service box, and vice versa.

e box

Different surfaces

Tennis was originally played on grass, but today surfaces range from cement and clay (outdoor) to wood and carpet (indoor).

Slow courts

Clay, all-weather tarmac and indoor rubber surfaces.

The ball bounces slowly and at a steep angle. It's best to use a baseline game (see page 19).

You will have a reasonable amount of time to prepare your shots.

Fast courts

Grass, cement, indoor carpet and artificial grass surfaces.

The ball bounces low and fast, skidding forward after bouncing. Try a serve and volley game (see page 19).

Watch out – you will have little time to play your shots.

5

Getting started

Before trying out any tennis strokes, there are some basic things to remember. You need to know how to hold the racket properly and how to get into a good position to hit the ball.

Right- or left-handed?

The instructions in this book are given for right-handed players, but can be reversed for left-handers.

For instance, right-handers play forehand strokes on the right, but left-handers play them on the left.

The racket

Here are the different parts of the racket. The middle of the racket face is called the "sweet spot". It will give you the most powerful shot.

Young players can use junior short-handle rackets. These give you more control of the racket head. As you improve, try using a junior racket of normal length.

Rackets should not feel top heavy. Hold the racket to find the correct grip size. Your thumb and second finger should overlap slightly.

Handle

Grip the handle near the end, comfortably and not too tightly.

Throat

Head

Face

Sweet spot

The ready position

Between every shot, return to the "ready" position, as shown here. You will then be able to move off quickly in any direction.

Hold the racket in a forehand grip, supporting it gently with your other hand.

Stand with your feet apart, your knees slightly bent and your weight forward on the balls of your feet.

Tips

Here are some general tips for playing good tennis.

- Try to develop a good technique for the three main types of shot:
  Groundstrokes (pages 8-9)
  Service (pages 10-11) and smash (page 15)
  Volleys (pages 12-13)

- Be quick on your feet. You may not have much time to get into the best position to play a shot.

- Keep your eye on the ball. You can then move into a good position to return it.

- Have confidence and keep up your concentration.

Tennis gear

Tennis clothes are traditionally white, but many players today wear clothes with different patterns and shades. Cotton clothes are best as they are comfortable and absorb sweat.

Running and turning puts strain on your feet. Wear lace-up, lightweight tennis shoes, with a good grip.

Groundstrokes

Groundstrokes are forehand and backhand drives –
long, powerful strokes, played with a swinging action
after the ball has bounced.

Forehand grip

Here is the most simple grip. Move your
hand around the handle until the "V"
between your palm and thumb joins up
with the right-hand ridge of the handle.

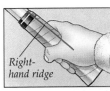

*Right-
hand ridge*

Forehand drive

1. For the forehand drive, as for every
tennis shot, start in the ready position
described on page 7.

2. Step to your right, turning your
shoulders with the weight on your right
foot. Swing the racket back and forward
smoothly.

3. Start swinging your racket up and
forward, keeping the swing long and
smooth. As you swing your racket,
transfer your weight onto your left foot.

4. Keep your wrist firm as your racket
approaches the ball. Hit the ball with your
racket at waist height and the racket head
at right angles to the ground.

5. Continue the forward swinging
action after you have hit the ball. This
is the "follow-through", finishing the
stroke in a smooth, controlled action.

Backhand grip

For the backhand grip, move your hand around the handle until the "V" of your hand joins up with the left-hand ridge.

Left-hand ridge

Backhand drive

1. Take your racket back in a shallow arc and turn your shoulders away from the net. Support the racket with your free hand.

2. Change to the backhand grip. Start swinging the racket forward. Step forward and across to your left with your right foot, transferring your weight onto it.

3. Bend your knees slightly as you step forward and swing the racket at the ball. Keep your wrist firm and swing your arm from the shoulder.

4. Continue the forward swinging action after you have hit the ball. This is the follow-through, finishing the stroke in a smooth, controlled action.

Double-handed backhand

• As a beginner tennis player, you will probably use two hands on the backhand drive. Use two forehand grips with your hands close together, right below left. Follow the instructions above as for a single-handed backhand.

• As you improve, use a backhand grip for the right hand and a forehand grip for the left.

Service

The first service of a game is played from the right-hand court. It then alternates after every point. If your first service is called out, you can make a second service.

Service grip

Use the forehand grip (see page 8) until you get the service action right. The best grip to use, however, is the "chopper" grip. This helps you to "throw" your racket at the ball properly.

Central plane

To find the chopper grip, the "V" of your hand should line up with the central plane of the handle.

The throw-up

Throwing the ball up well makes a big difference to your service. Throw the ball up, so that if you were to let it bounce, it would land about 30cm (1ft) in front of your left toes.

Throw the ball up a little higher than you can reach with your racket at full stretch, so you can hit it just as it starts to fall.

If your feet cross or touch the baseline before you have served, a "foot fault" is called. The service counts against you.*

Service action

The service is the only shot in which you have complete control over the timing and positioning of the ball. Here's how to serve.

1. Stand side-on to the net, with feet apart and your left foot 10cm (4in) from the baseline. Hold the ball in your left hand.

2. Take your racket around behind your back. At the same time, throw the ball straight up into the air with your left hand.

3. As you bring your racket up to hit the ball, start pushing up onto your toes so that you get your whole weight behind the shot.

4. As your racket comes over your head, snap your wrist forward to give you extra power. This is the "throwing" action.

5. Make sure that you don't commit a foot fault (see bottom of page 10). Hit the ball at the highest point you can reach.

6. Follow through the service's forward motion. Finish with the racket down your left-hand side and your weight forward.

Volleys

Volleys are short, quick strokes played by punching your racket at the ball before it bounces. You put opponents under pressure because they have less time to prepare for the next shot.

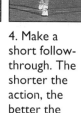

Forehand volley

1. As for all your tennis shots, start in the ready position. Keep your eye on the ball.

2. Turn around so that your left shoulder is pointing at the net, with your weight on your right foot.

3. Step foward with your left foot. Punch your racket at the ball. Don't let the racket head drop.

4. Make a short follow-through. The shorter the action, the better the volley.

Backhand volley

1. Start in the ready position, as before. Keep your eye on the ball and prepare to move off.

2. Turn so that your right shoulder is pointing at the net. Support the racket with your free hand.

3. Step forward with your right foot. Punch the racket at the ball, keeping the racket head flat.

4. As with the forehand volley, make a short follow-through to help control the ball.

Going to the net

To give yourself time to move to the net to volley, play a deep shot down the sideline or across the court. This may force your opponent to play a weak return, which you can volley away from them.

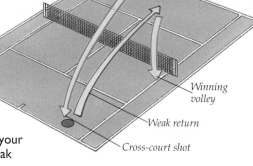

Winning volley

Weak return

Cross-court shot

When at the net, if your racket hits it during or after the shot, you lose the point.

Adapting the volley

Ideally, you should play a volley between shoulder and hip height, but you may need to adapt your stroke for high and low balls.

For low volleys, bend your knees so that the ball is almost at eye level. Then punch it up.

Half-volley

You will see professionals play half-volleys. These are defensive shots which need a lot of practice. The player hits the ball at the very moment that it hits the ground. There is hardly a noticeable bounce.

Hit high volleys by hitting the ball down.

Tips

- Use the same grip as for forehand and backhand drives. As you improve, you may feel that you can volley with just one grip.*
- Keep your wrist firm and your racket steady.
- Don't swing your racket. A short punching action and a short follow-through are the keys to a good volley.

*See pages 8-9 for forehand and backhand grips.

13

The lob and the smash

The lob is a defensive shot and the smash is an attacking one. The lob is used to return the smash and vice-versa.

Using the lob

The lob is fairly easy, but you need to place the ball carefully. Try to play it deep with plenty of height into your opponent's half of the court.

A lob can force opponents away from an attacking position near the net.

The smash

This is one of the most exciting shots to play. When the ball is high in the air, you hit it down hard.

This girl is about to sweep the ball up into the air for a backhand lob.

A deep lob gives you time to recover under pressure.

Lob tips

- For the forehand lob, see page 15. For the backhand lob, change your grip and turn your shoulders.

- Don't forget to swing your racket at the ball.

Forehand lob

Try to play a lob to make it travel high over your opponent's head, landing just inside the baseline.

1. For this shot, take your racket back and turn on your right foot.

2. Step in with your left foot, bringing your racket forward and up.

3. Hit the ball when opposite your front hip. Tilt the racket to lift the ball.

4. Make your follow-through high, ending with the racket above your head.

Forehand smash

Hit hard and fast.

1. Turn on your right foot. With your racket back, point up at the ball.

2. Bring your racket up, to "throw" it at the ball (see page 11).

3. Reach up and hit the ball at the highest point that you can reach.

4. End your follow-through with your racket down by your side.

Smash tips

- The best grip is the "chopper" grip (page 10). At first, if you find it easier, try groundstroke grips (pages 8-9).

- Get into position quickly by side-stepping across court.

Using spin

When you feel confident with your basic shots, you can use spin to add variety. This makes the ball more difficult to return. The shots shown here are based on the actions for groundstrokes and the service.*

This girl is playing a sliced backhand.

Different types of spin

There are two main types of spin – topspin and slice. They both change the way the ball travels through the air and how it bounces (though this also depends on what surface you are playing on).

A basic hit

If you play a shot with a firm, forward hit, the ball will spin slightly. This kind of shot will give you power and also some control over where the ball lands.

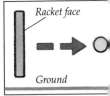

Racket face

Ground

Topspin

Topspin gives speed and more control. The racket head brushes up and over the ball. It forces the ball down so you can hit it higher (and more safely) over the net. The ball bounces high and "kicks forward".

Hitting direction

Slice

The racket head brushes down and underneath the ball. Slice takes the speed off the ball and gives control. The ball dips in the air and stays low. It skids low and bounces back away from your opponent.

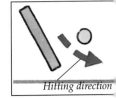

Hitting direction

See pages 8-9 for how to hold your racket.

When to use spin

Use spin to upset your opponent's rhythm in a long baseline rally. He or she will find it harder to anticipate your next shot. Use heavy topspin for better ball control, gaining accuracy without losing speed. Use slice to counter topspin from your opponent.

Topspin is useful on a second service*. It gives greater control and reliability.

Use spin to disguise shots. Prepare as for a groundstroke, but add topspin or slice.

Play a sliced backhand if your opponent's ball falls in the middle of the court. Then run in to attack.

Drop shots

Drop shots are delicate, sliced shots that need excellent racket control. They can be played on the forehand or backhand. They are often used to break up long rallies by aiming the ball to land just over the net.

1. Prepare as if for a forehand drive. Take the racket back and step across with your left leg.

2. Bring the racket forward and brush down, under the ball.

3. Don't forget to make your follow-through in the direction of the moving ball.

*See page 10.

Playing a match

Winning a tennis match relies on planning, tactics and mental attitude, as much as it relies on good, powerful shots. Here are some tips to help you win!*

Know your game

Get to know your own strengths and weaknesses by asking yourself some questions. For instance, which shots do you find most difficult or which shots lose you the most points? Base your game around your most accurate and reliable shots.

If you aren't very fit, you may have to play a defensive game from the baseline.

Wrong-foot your opponent. Start with a regular hitting pattern. As your opponent moves for your next shot, hit it in the opposite direction.

Are you a baseliner who is good at groundstrokes, or a good server and volleyer who attacks well at the net? (See page 19.)

Work out beforehand how you would like the match to go. You could prepare a written match plan.

Opponent has weak, sliced backhand.
Attack backhand with service.
Take advantage of weak, defensive return to get to the net to volley.

Coping with nerves

Feeling nervous stops you from playing well. Relax by taking deep breaths as you prepare to serve or to return service.

If your opponent looks nervous and tense, put this to your advantage. Use your tactics to force him or her to make errors.

Tennis tactics

There are two main styles of play – baseline play, and serve and volley play. In baseline play, games are mainly made up of long groundstroke rallies from the baseline. The idea is to keep the ball in play until you see an opportunity for a winning shot.

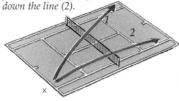

Catch your opponent out, by varying your shots. Try going cross-court (1) or down the line (2).

In serve and volley play, the idea is to run into the net after serving, to attack with a volley. This means that your serve must be strong. Once you decide to go into the net, don't change your mind. You could get stranded in no-man's land.

Play a deep, fast service (1). Your opponent's return may be weak (2). You can then play a winning volley (3).

Tips

- Learn to combine serve and volley play with baseline play.

- After each shot, return to a central position to cover both sides of the court. In baseline play, go to the middle of the baseline. If you are volleying, stand 3m (9ft) from the middle of the net.

- If you are under pressure, just aim to keep the ball in play until you can gain an advantage.

Unforced errors

Many points can be lost when a player makes avoidable mistakes. Players do this due to lack of concentration or control. These are called "unforced errors".

Serving and returning

Serving and returning service are two of the most important shots in tennis. They can immediately put you in a strong position – or not! Here's how to play these two shots in a match.

Where to stand to serve

The first point in a game is served from the right-hand box. For each point, you then continue serving from alternate boxes. You usually serve to your opponent's backhand.

Serving from the right

Stand just behind the baseline, right of the centre mark. Serve almost straight down the centre service line.

Serving from the left

Stand just behind the baseline, left of the centre mark. Aim for the far right of the service box.

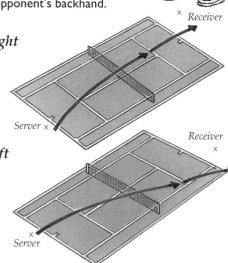

Serving tips

- At first, concentrate on serving accurately rather than fast.
- To keep your opponent guessing, vary your serving. Aim mostly to the backhand, but occassionally serve wide to the forehand.
- You should generally serve more slowly on the second service to make sure that the ball goes in.
- Serve deep to force your opponent to play weak returns.

Returning service

Returning well is just as important as serving. To win a match, you need to win at least one of the games your opponent is serving, in each set. This is known as "breaking serve".

Where to stand to return

Where you stand will be affected by the speed of your opponent's service, but here is a guideline. For a fast service, stand 1m (3ft) behind the baseline (Return 1). Move forward to return a second service (Return 2).

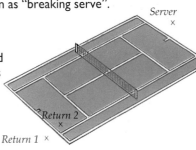

Server
×

Return 2
×

Return 1 ×

Blocked and chipped returns

These are adaptations of groundstroke returns. They have short backswings which give you more time to play the shot. Blocked returns are good against fast services. Chipped returns are good against topspin.

Chipped return. Hit the ball firmly with slice.

Blocked return. Punch the racket at the ball after it has bounced.

Returning tips

- You must react quickly to the service – a ball moving at 96kmph (60mph) will reach you in one second. Some top players serve at over 200kmph (125mph).

- Keep your knees and body slightly bent with your weight forward, in case you have to move forward or back to receive the ball.

- Force the server to make mistakes by returning reliably.

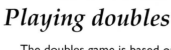

Playing doubles

The doubles game is based on teamwork. It is mainly an attacking, serve and volley game, so you need to get to the net fast.

You and your partner

Your partner's game should be strong where yours is weak and vice-versa. Give yourselves scores out of five for each aspect of your game. The ideal total should be between seven and ten.

Key	Aspect of game	You	Friend	Total
5 Excellent	Service	4	4	8
4 Very good	Forehand	5	2	7
3 Good	Backhand	3	5	8
2 Fair	Volley	5	5	10
1 Weak	Temperament	2	5	7

Positions on court

Here is where players stand to start a point when the service is from the right of the court. For the next point, the server and partner change sides. The receiver moves forward and his or her partner moves back to return serve.

Receiver

Receiver's partner stands 1m (3ft) inside service line, and 2m (6ft) from centre line.

Server

Server's partner stands in the middle of the service box.

Going to the net

The aim of both doubles teams is to get to the net as quickly as possible and attack. This forces their opponents to stay back on the baseline.

In top-class matches, you may see all four players volleying at the net. These net rallies are so fast that volleys are often played just by instinct. These are known as "reflex" volleys.

Teamwork strategy

Always stay alert while your partner is playing the ball. Be ready to cover the rest of the court and hit the shot if he or she misses it.

Cover your partner in case he or she misses the shot.

To confuse your opponents, move slightly as if you are about to hit the ball, then move back again while your partner plays the shot. This is called feinting.

Communication

To play well as a team, you must communicate with your partner so that you both know what to do. To avoid getting in each other's way or both leaving a ball, work out a system of simple calls, like these:

"Mine" – you have more chance of hitting a good shot than your partner.

"Yours" – your partner has a better chance.

A hidden signal stops your opponents from guessing your tactics.

23

Tennis practice

Exercises can develop your confidence, technique and ball sense. Try the ones on this page by yourself, and those opposite with a partner.

Shadow stroking

This is a good way to try out groundstrokes. Go through the motions of the shot, correcting yourself if you do anything wrong.

Improve your forehand

Net height

Hit balls against a wall. Mark a chalk line on the wall, about 1m (3ft) above net height. Aim forehand drives at just above the line.

Hit the target

To make your service more accurate, try putting targets, such as tin cans or racket covers, in the far corners of each service court. Aim to hit each target in turn.

Punch the ball

Chalk a circle on a wall. Then stand about 2m (6ft) away and volley balls at it to develop your punching action. Try ten forehand volleys and then ten backhand volleys.

Concentrate on turning your shoulders.

Down the line

Playing "down the line" rallies with a friend improves your groundstroke accuracy. One of you hits forehands down the sidelines, while the other hits backhands. Do ten shots each and then swap over.

Positioning

To work on your body positioning, ask a friend to hit balls to your forehand, slightly away from you. You have to move into the right position to play the shot.

This speeds up your reactions.

Volley targets

To improve the placing of your volleys, ask a friend to hit balls to you. Volley them to certain target areas, for example, deep into the corners of the court or at short angles across the court.

Lobs and smashes

Working on lobs and smashes with a partner is a good way to improve your control of these shots. One of you hits up lobs, while the other returns with a smash. Then change around.

Adding spin

Ask a friend to hit balls to you and return them using a sequence of shots, such as the one shown here.

1. Basic forehand drive

2. Sliced backhand

3. Topspin forehand

Fitness and injury

To play good tennis, you need to build up your fitness as well as your technique. Building up your strength and stamina may also help you to avoid injury.

Warming up and down

Always warm up before a match or training session, and then warm down again after it. This loosens your muscles so that you don't strain them. Do each of these exercises five times.

With your hands on your hips, lean back from your waist, keeping your legs straight. Then rotate your upper body in a circle.

Stand with your feet apart and your left arm raised. Bend to the right, then straighten up slowly. Repeat for the other side.

Stand and shake out your hands and arms for a few seconds. Then rotate your arms in ten forward circles. Then do ten backward ones.

Tennis injuries

Tennis players can suffer from many types of injury, from blisters and pulled muscles to tennis elbow. This is an inflammation of the elbow, sometimes caused by the constant mis-timing of shots. For any injuries apart from minor cuts and bruises, always consult your doctor.

Improve your speed

You can build up your speed and the way you move around the court by doing some shuttle sprints.

Put three balls on the singles sidelines, about 10cm (4in) apart. Stand behind the opposite sideline, then sprint across the court, pick up one ball, turn quickly and sprint back. Put the ball on the sideline and repeat for the other two.

As you get fitter, increase the number of balls.

Stand with your legs wide apart. Lunge to your left, bending your left knee but keeping your right leg straight. Straighten up and repeat the same exercise to your right.

Stand up straight, then bend down slowly and touch your toes. Straighten up slowly, keeping your legs straight.

To avoid injury

- Always warm up and down properly.
- Build up your training slowly. Don't do too much to start with.
- If you feel pain, stop exercising. Treat injuries as soon as they happen and allow time for them to heal.

Tennis history

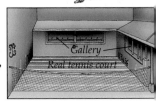

Today's game of tennis developed from the ancient indoor game of "royal" or "real" tennis. During the 1800s, people experimented with different versions of the game. Some of these games became the forerunners of today's game.

Real tennis

Real tennis was first played by the nobility in France in the 1200s. It is played over a net, but the court has "galleries" or ledges around its walls, which are part of the playing area, like the walls of a squash court.

Gallery

Real tennis court

Famous dates

1872 First known lawn tennis club is founded.

1874 Englishman Major Clopton Wingfield introduces a popular version of tennis called *spharistiké*, or "sticky" for short. This was the basis of today's game.

1875 First known set of rules are drawn up.

1877 The All-England Croquet Club becomes the All-England Croquet and Lawn Tennis Club. In July it holds the first Wimbledon championships (men's singles only). The winner is Spencer William Gore.

1878 Overarm service is first used.

1881 First US championships are held (men's singles only).

1884 First men's doubles and first women's singles are played at Wimbledon.

1887 First women's singles are played at the US championships.

The Grand Slam

The highest achievement in professional tennis is to win the Grand Slam – the top four championships in the same year. The championships are the Australian Open, the French Open, Wimbledon and the US Open. As the tournaments are played on a variety of surfaces, the winner has to be a great all-rounder.

The plate awarded to the Wimbledon women's champion.

1891 First French championships are held.

1896 The first modern Olympic Games are held, at which tennis is played. Tennis remains an Olympic sport until 1924. It is reintroduced in 1988.

1900 First Davis Cup is held. It is played between Britain and the USA.

1905 First Australian championships.

1913 First women's and mixed doubles are played at Wimbledon.

1922 Seeding is first introduced at the US championships. Wimbledon changes from a challenge tournament (where the previous year's winner plays in the final) to a knock-out tournament.

1968 "Open" tennis begins, in which professionals (who play for a living) can take part with amateurs.

1970 The tie-break is introduced.

How to score

Here you can find out how to score. A match is divided up into sets, and sets are divided into games.

Game...

The points in a game are 15, 30, 40, then game. To win a game, you must win these four points and also be two points clear of your opponent. If the score reaches 40-40, or "deuce", the next point scored is called "advantage". If the player who has scored an advantage then loses the next point, the score goes back to deuce. If the player wins it, he or she wins the game.

Set...

The first player to win six games by a margin of at least two games, for example 6-4, wins the set. If the score reaches 6-6, the tie-break is used (see below).

...and Match!

To win a match, you normally have to win the best of three sets. Men play the best of five sets in major tournaments.

The tie-break

Tie-breaks are played when the score in a set reaches 6-6. Points are scored as 1, 2, 3 and so on. The first player to win seven points with a margin of at least two points wins the set. If the score in the tie-break becomes 6-6, play continues until one player reaches a two-point lead.

The player who serves first in a normal set, serves the first point of the tie-break. The players then serve two points each alternately.

Some basic rules

For more detail, look at a tennis rule book.

1. Service
- At the start of the match, a coin is tossed. The winner of the toss can choose who serves first, or which end to play from.

- The server must stand behind the baseline and between the centre mark and the sideline. The ball must land in the service box opposite to the side the server is serving from.

- The server's feet must not touch or cross the baseline until after the ball has been hit. If they do, a foot fault has been made and the service is disallowed.

- A service fault is called if: the server misses the ball as he or she tries to hit it; the ball touches the net and then lands outside the service box; the ball lands in the wrong service box.

- A player has two chances to serve on each point. If a fault is called after the first service, a second service is allowed. If both are out, the point is lost.

- A "let" is called if the ball hits the net and then lands in the correct service box. If this happens on the first serve, you still have two serves left. If it happens on the second serve, you have only one serve left.

- The players must serve alternate games.

2. Changing ends
- Players change ends of the court after the first game and then after every two games. In a tie-break, they change ends every six points.

3. How the server wins points
- The server wins the point if the receiver does not return the ball back into the court.

4. How the receiver wins points
- The receiver wins points if the server serves a double fault; that is, both services are called as faults.

5. How players lose points

- If the ball bounces twice before they hit it.

- If the ball lands out of court or in the net.

- If they catch or carry their ball on their racket or their racket touches the ball more than once while playing a shot.

- If their racket or clothing touches the net, the posts or the ground in their opponent's court while the ball is in play.

- If they volley the ball before it is on their side of the net.

- If the ball touches them or their clothing.

- If they throw (release) their racket in order to hit the ball.

Index

Acknowledgements

The publishers would like to thank the following for permission to
reproduce their photographs.
Cover, Professional Sport International; p3 and p29, Allsport; p5 top
right, Wimbledon Lawn Tennis Museum; p7, p10, p14, Sporting
Pictures (UK) Ltd.

This book is based on material previously published in *Improve Your Tennis Skills*. First
published in 1996 by Usborne Publishing Ltd, Usborne House, 83-85 Saffron Hill, London,
EC1N 8RT. Copyright © Usborne Publishing Ltd 1989, 1993, 1996.